D1105481

Cayer

All By Myself

All By Myself

Anna Grossnickle Hines

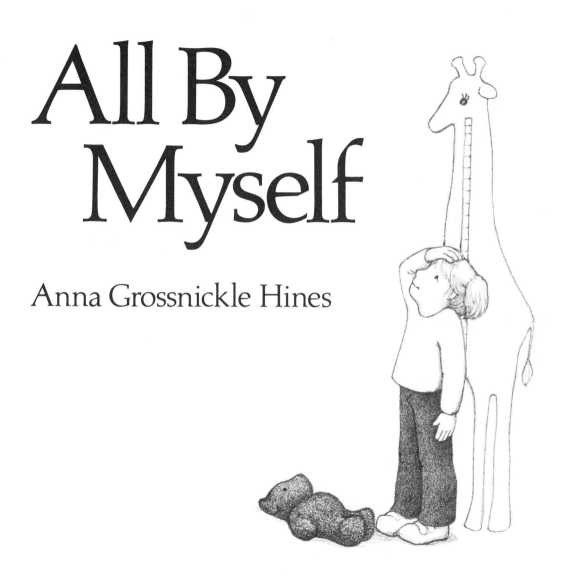

Clarion Books/Ticknor & Fields: A Houghton Mifflin Company/New York

For Lassen, all by herself

Clarion Books
Ticknor & Fields, a Houghton Mifflin Company
Copyright © 1985 by Anna Grossnickle Hines

All rights reserved. No part of this work may be reproduced
or transmitted in any form or by any means, electronic or
mechanical, including photocopying and recording, or by any
information storage or retrieval system, except as may be
expressly permitted by the 1976 Copyright Act or in writing
by the publisher. Requests for permission should be addressed
in writing to Clarion Books, 52 Vanderbilt Avenue, New York, NY 10017.
Printed in the U.S.A.

Library of Congress Cataloging in Publication Data
Hines, Anna Grossnickle.
All by myself.

Summary: One night, for the first time, Josie has
to cross the dark bedroom to go to the bathroom all
by herself.
1. Children's stories, American. 1. Self-reliance—
Fiction] I. Title
PZ7.H572Al 1985   [E]   84-19882
ISBN 0-89919-293-9

Y 10 9 8 7 6 5 4 3 2 1

"When I was a teensy-weensy little baby," Josie said,
"how did I eat?"
"I had to feed you," Mama said.
"Now I can eat all by myself," said Josie.

"How did I wash my hands when I was a baby?"
"I did it for you."
"Not any more though. Right, Mama? Now I do it
 all by myself."

"Did you brush my teeth, too?"
"You didn't have any teeth to brush."
Josie laughed. The thought of no teeth was funny.

"How did I go to the bathroom?"
"You didn't go to the bathroom at all," Mama said.
"You wore diapers all the time."

"Well, not any more. Now I can go to the bathroom
all by myself."
Except at nighttime.
At nighttime Mama still put diapers on Josie.

"I hate diapers!" Josie said. "I want panties. I can put panties
 on all by myself."
"But you might wet your bed while you are sleeping,"
 Mama said.

"No, I won't. I'll wake up," said Josie. "I want to do it
all by myself."
"All right," Mama agreed.

Josie put on her panties and pajamas and went to bed.

She woke up in the big dark night. She had that funny
too-full feeling.
"Mama," she called.
Mama came and turned on the light. Josie went to
the bathroom.

In the morning she hopped out of her cozy dry bed. "I did it," she said, "all by myself."

"That's good," Mama said. "No more diapers for you."

But that night Josie didn't wake up. In the morning everything was wet.

"Is it too hard to wake up?" Mama asked. "You could have
 diapers again if you want."
"No!" Josie said. "No more diapers for me. I can do it
 all by myself."
"All right," Mama said, "but you'll have to wake up."

That night Josie woke up. Did she have that funny feeling?
She wasn't sure, but she called Mama anyway.

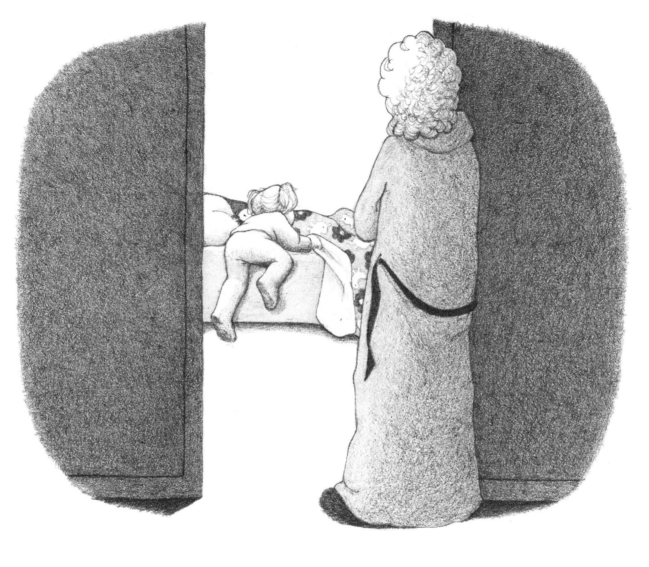

Mama came and turned on the light. Josie went into the
bathroom, but nothing happened. She crawled into bed
and went back to sleep.

Soon she was awake again. She called Mama to turn on the light so she could go to the bathroom a second time.

Josie woke up again and again,

all through the night.

In the morning she said, "No wet bed! No more
diapers for me."
Mama yawned. "No more diapers," she said.

That night Josie was very tired. Mama was tired, too. Josie put on her panties and pajamas and went to bed.

She woke up in the middle of the night. She had that funny
feeling. She called Mama to turn on the light but Mama
didn't come. Josie called again, but Mama was too tired to
wake up.

Josie sat in her cozy dry bed and looked out into the big dark night.
She didn't want a wet bed. She didn't want any more diapers.

She put her feet down onto the floor. Slowly she walked across the big dark room.

Carefully she felt in the darkness for her little stool. Slowly
and carefully she climbed up and turned on the light.

Josie went to the bathroom all by herself.

In her room she stepped up onto the stool and turned off
the light.
Carefully she crossed the dark room and climbed back into
her cozy bed.

In the morning Josie jumped out of bed. "I did it!" she said.
"This time I REALLY did it all by myself!"
"You really did!" said Mama.

"When I was a teensy-weensy little baby," Josie said, "how did
I get on your lap for hugs and stories?"
"I had to pick you up," Mama said.

"Well, not any more," said Josie.